Zoila the Zebra's WOW!
(Words of Wisdom)

By
Juanita Quinones Gandara
Mark Bowles
Illustrated by Christopher Dart

ISBN 978-1984962317 First Edition

Dedication from Juanita:
I'd like to dedicate this book in memory of a best father a young girl could have had, (Prudenciano "Chano" Quinones), my mother (Natalia Quinones Soto), my boys (Mark Andrew and Matthew Robert Gandara), my first grandchild (Adreena Faith Gandara) referred to as, my "mamacita mama" and her twin siblings due in May 2018! (Lexi Rose and Liam Hernandez), (Azayzel Paige Gandara), (John B. Howell), and to all my future grandchildren! Also, I dedicate this book to my dear siblings (Blanca Gallegos, Sylvia Gallardo, and Eddie Quinonez), family and friends, whom I truly love and care for. I'd also like to give credit to all the beautiful educators, children, students, parents and communities who crossed my path and whom I was fortunate enough to serve and get to know. Thank you for always allowing me to feel that I was "Blessed to be a blessing!"

Dedication from Mark:
To my father, Donald, whose stories of the daring half-a-worm inspired the imagination of a little boy. Also, to my mother, Joan, who first took that little boy to the children's section of a library and shared the joy of reading each night.

They would both like to give a special thanks to Gina Crawford for her writing expertise and advice, Connie Vela for her support and coordination, and Amy Freels for her design and publication insight.

**Friends and amigos,
hello and hola!
I am a zebra,
and my name is
Zoila.**

Hola is Spanish for **hello**,
and an **amigo** is a **friend**!
I am Armando the Armadillo,
and I am Zoila's best amigo!

A talking zebra
did you say?
You don't see one
of those every day!

I suppose you do not **hear** one either!

**Your observation
is quite true.
This makes me special,
just like you!**

We are all special.
It is a fun game to find out how.
Let's play!

Although you don't have
black and white stripes,
I like making friends
of ALL different types!

No two zebra patterns are the same.
Do you like Zoila's?

I'm so glad we have
this chance to meet.
Let's share
how we are unique!

I say, **"you"** nique, and **"me"** nique.
Get it? I am a funny armadillo!

I will begin with my autobiography,
then please tell me yours.
I will listen carefully
sitting on all fours.

An **autobiography** is a unique story only you can tell about yourself!

My mother is a homemaker, music lover, great cook, and baker!

Our food is healthy and organic. Our family is proudly Hispanic.

Hispanics are people who originate from a Spanish culture.

My father builds rock-climbing walls, with safety ropes to prevent falls.

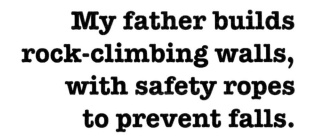

He owns and manages his very own business. He works so hard to promote health and fitness!

Never climb without an adult, especially if you have hooves instead of hands like Zoila!

I was born in
Cd. Juarez, Chihuahua Mexico.
We always yearned
to live in the grand city of El Paso.

My family and I
have always been a team.
Together we sought
the American Dream!

The **American Dream** means that through hard work, everyone has the same opportunity to succeed.

The day to depart
finally came,
I was so excited
I didn't complain.

My dad and mom
packed up our car.
I held my favorite doll, "Pipa!"
though we didn't drive far.

The United States flag has
50 stars and 13 red and white stripes.
Hey, the flag has stripes like Zoila!

We drove over
the Rio Grande river.
I clung to Pipa tightly
because I am not a great swimmer.

We travelled across
a giant road in the sky.
It was the Bridge of the Americas
though I pretended to fly.

The **Rio Grande** is a Spanish term
meaning **big river**, and is the fourth
longest river in the United States.

I said, "Zoom, zoom"
imagining my legs were wings.
I dreamed of soaring into the clouds
where I could twirl and sing.

Once we crossed
to the American shore,
my daydream ended
and I was ready to explore!

The Rio Grande is called
Rio Bravo in Mexico.
That means **furious river**.

In Texas, we made
our new home!
Though at first,
I felt small and alone.

I left all my friends
in Mexico behind.
I hoped I would soon
find someone kind!

Texas is the second largest state.
Alaska is the biggest.
Rhode Island is the smallest.
Big and small are equally important!

My parents said,
"Zoila, Amorcito corazon,
don't worry!
You will make amigos
in a hurry."

I was so nervous the first day.
I even thought
I might forget
how to play!

Amorcito Corazon is like saying **sweetheart**. We already learned **amigo** is the word for **friend**.

Will you be our amigo?

I was afraid of bullies
And all who were mean.
The tears in my blue eyes
glistened and gleamed.

I took a deep breath,
and to my parents confessed,
"Don't worry padrecitos,
I will do MY VERY best!"

Padrecitos are **parents**.
They told her,
"As long as you are trying your best,
you will never fail."

As I was walking to
my bus,
I felt like running away
and making a fuss!

Under the Texas sun
blew the hot El Paso breeze.
And in that moment,
I had an epiphany!

An **epiphany** is an ah-ha moment when
you get an answer to a question or have
a great idea.

I said to myself,
"I will be strong and lead!"
"If anyone is bullied,
I will help with great speed."

"I will be myself,
on whom others can depend."
"If someone is hurt or sad,
I will quickly befriend."

Bullies intimidate and hurt others.
This makes me so sad!

It didn't take long,
and as I took action,
my "caring" soon started
a chain reaction.

Being true to myself
helped me make friends galore!
And one by one,
the bullies were no more.

A **chain reaction** is like a falling line of dominoes. Hey, dominoes are black and white like my friend Zoila!

Bullies no more?
But how?
It really is simple.
You just have to yell, "WOW!"

Why **WOW**? Let me explain.

Sure, you could shout:
Far out!
Whoa!
Que padre!
Cool!
or Holy Cow!
But I like the sound
of **WOW!**

The sound a wild zebra makes is a high-pitched bark, roar, and snort. It sounds like **que padre**, which means **how cool**!

What's the secret?
Listen up! Here it is.
You never know;
there might be a
quiz!

WOW stands for
Zoila the Zebra's

Words **O**f **W**isdom

It is the key,
my recipe,
my way to live
bully free!

Let's practice **WOW**! Here we go!
We will show you how!

WOW #1
is the "Golden Rule."
Those who follow it
have the perfect tool.

If you treat others the way
you want to be treated,
you will never, ever
feel defeated.

If we treat everyone with respect,
we are more likely to be respected too.

**WOW #2
is to "Be your best self!"
Be humble, kind,
and share your wealth.**

**If you take turns
and play nice with all,
you will be looked up to,
even if you're small.**

By **wealth** we mean if you have
two blue crayons, share one!

WOW #3
is "If you feel angry,
stop and think!"
Take a moment to calm down
and quietly blink.

Inhale a deep breath,
breathe out slowly, count to ten
and you will soon find
peace again.

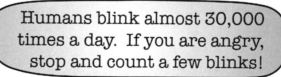

Humans blink almost 30,000 times a day. If you are angry, stop and count a few blinks!

WOW #4
is "Communication is key!"
This makes me so happy
when we speak honestly.

If you do something wrong,
have courage and communicate.
Apologize and be strong!
Saying "I'm sorry" feels great!

Lo siento is Spanish for *I'm sorry*.

Hablando se entiende la gente
Means *communication is key*.

WOW #5
is to "Be a good listener."
This is the quickest path
to becoming a winner.

Listen to your family,
friends, and teachers.
This is often considered
a person's best feature.

Listening is a great way to make new friends!

The story of my journey
is now at the end.

Now tell me yours!
Let's be friends!

This is my secret
and not one to keep.
Take it, run,
shout, and leap!

Watch the chain reaction
from my little word.
When you shout and share it,
WOW will be seen and heard!

Can you say acronym? Each letter of an
acronym stands for a different word.
WOW is **Words of Wisdom**.
TAG is **Treat Amigos Great**.

Made in the USA
Columbia, SC
23 June 2020